Love of the Father

David Hollier

xulon PRESS

Copyright © 2011 by David A. Hollier

Love of the Father
by David A. Hollier

Printed in the United States of America

ISBN 9781612157634

All rights reserved solely by the author. The author guarantees all contents are original and do not infringe upon the legal rights of any other person or work. No part of this book may be reproduced in any form without the permission of the author. The views expressed in this book are not necessarily those of the publisher.

Unless otherwise indicated, Bible quotations are taken from The New American Bible. Copyright © 1970 by Catholic Bible Publishers Wichita, Kansas 67201. Edition 1991-1992.

www.xulonpress.com

Table of Contents

Chapter 1:	Parents Nightmare	7
Chapter 2:	Unwanted Stranger...	15
Chapter 3:	A Dream...	37
Chapter 4:	Reflection...	53
Chapter 5:	Mark Goes to Church...	64
Chapter 6:	A Second Warning	81
Chapter 7:	A Son's Sickness, a Father's Test	93
Chapter 8:	A Family's Grief	104
Chapter 9:	The Man on the Bench	116
Chapter 10:	The Conversation	132
Chapter 11:	Jesus and the Dad	137
Chapter 12:	God's Promise Made Good	143

Chapter 1

Parents Nightmare

Driving down the cool California highway early in the morning was something Jason always enjoyed. It was hard to beat the California bay area weather that made Oakland unique, 68 degrees in July without a cloud in the sky. Long ago he might have felt that the good Lord had blessed him by letting him live in such a beautiful place. Now he knew it was just his good fortune.

There was little traffic on the interstate this early on a Monday morning. An early start put him a step ahead and spared him the stress of a congested interstate which always tested his patience. Jason liked to stay in motion. Even at work, he could not stand for someone to lag behind in their work.

Jason had taken over Bright Idea, a computer and software company, from his father, Jason Albright II after he took sick and could no longer work. Running the family business was something Jason had dreamed of as far back as he could remember. He had long relished the challenge of keeping Bright Idea on top.

Bright Idea was founded by Jason Albright I, beginning first as a hobby he enjoyed in his garage. It became his business when he envisioned a day beyond room-sized computers, to when they would become a part of everyday life. In no time, Bright Idea Computers outgrew the garage, then a simple office, to its present day operation that enjoyed an international presence, employing three thousand people in the US and abroad.

Jason Albright III was a very smart, capable young man who, family connection aside, was the

Love of the Father

best choice to take the helm of Bright Idea. In fact, the company was Jason's passion, and 12-14 hour workdays were the norm, though he was also married, with children. He would readily admit he was no candidate for father of the year, but he provided for his family and his stay-at-home wife, Maria, was a fine mother.

Jason and Maria are in their fifteenth year of marriage. Maria is of Spanish descent, a petite brunette with a light olive complexion and blue eyes that sparkled. His heart nearly stopped the first time he saw her, and to this day Jason believes she could grace the cover of any beauty magazine. Besides being smart and energetic, she is a loving mother to their three children: Jason Jr. (IV), twelve; Mark, age ten, and; Donna, the "baby" at age 8.

Jason arrived at work early as it was the fifth, the day after the Independence Day holiday. He was always early since it set a good example for the staff. It had been a hectic holiday weekend. Plenty of time to relax when I retire, he thought to himself—something he often said to Mari and friends. Upon entering the parking garage, he handed a tip to the young man at the gate, something he always did. Jason had long ago decided that when he was in charge of the company, he would set things up the way he wanted, regardless of the outcome. One of his values was treating the staff well, a value he stressed to his managers. Although this was a challenge with a company the size of Bright Idea, Jason knew it was in the best interest of the company long term.

Both his father and grandfather had been more concerned about the work than the people behind it—his father most of all. Jason always rolled his eyes when his dad would say things like, "Son, never be too nice to the people that work for you—they may just stab you in the back for it." Jason's grandfather was not very personable with his employees, but he at least gave them bonuses. That stopped when his eyes closed forever.

Walking through the front door, Jason was greeted with a chorus of "Good morning Mr. Albright, did

Love of the Father

you have a nice weekend?" After nods and brief words of greeting, he strode into his office and was met immediately by his efficient executive assistant, Ms. Deborah Moreland. She had come to Bright Idea by way of Microsoft. She was in her mid-twenties, intelligent, multi-tasking dynamo whom Jason considered indispensable.

"You have several calls this morning Mr. Albright," Deborah said in a soft but business-like voice, holding out an impressive stack of messages.

"Man this is going to be a long day," Jason muttered as he took the messages from her and headed for his office.

The first message, marked "#1 URGENT!!" was from James Meyer, a partner in Meyer-Jones, a venture capital and investment conglomerate. This was a call he did not want to return. Ever since he personally negotiated a deal to outfit their large firm with the latest in Bright Idea computer, networking, and videoconferencing technology, Meyer had been bugging Jason about expanding his financial horizons.

Jason had no interest in spending another half hour being pitched, but knew he was destined for it—Meyer was well connected in business circles and a good "friend" to have.

After spending a half hour on the phone with Meyer, it took Jason only thirty minutes to breeze through the most important calls. Bright Idea was going through some challenges and all of them weighed on Jason's mind as he returned the calls. Wouldn't it be great, he thought, if one of these people had a solution or answer for even one of these challenges. This hope provided him a little more motivation. But after completing the calls, his hope was unrealized.

Just as Jason finished his last call, Deborah walked in.

"Jason, Maria is on line 2."

Jason nodded at her, pressed the line and put the receiver to his ear.

"Yes?" he said, a little more sharply than he meant—he was in business mode and his to-do list was long.

Love of the Father

"Hello darling," Maria said in her sweet, tender voice, not seeming to notice his tense response. "I am taking the kids to the mall and was just wondering if you needed anything," she asked.

"No, nothing," said Jason. Why was she calling about a mall trip?

"I expect we'll be there for a while. It's just me, Jason, and Mark since Donna is over at Becky's house. The boys are going to connect with some friends at the game room while I shop."

That got Jason's attention. Something about the mall and the kids that hung out there made him uncomfortable with the boys being unsupervised.

"I have to pick up some things from Sears and we may see a movie too. The boys just needed to get out of the house awhile—"

"Maria, I am really not comfortable with the boys being dropped off at the game room. Really strange people hang out there, and—"

"Jason the boys are ten and twelve now. It's been quite a while since I've done something just me and them. I want it to be fun for them. Besides, you always say they need to be more responsible and independent. This is how they learn to be."

Jason still had concerns, but he knew she was right—and the to-do list was coming back to his mind.

"Alright, but please go over all the 'stranger' stuff with them keep an eye on them and don't leave them for very long."

"No problem," Maria said with a chuckle. "As an experienced mom, I am sure I can handle it."

Jason tended to be more concerned about those kinds of things than Maria. Despite her husband's name and position, she was committed to giving her kids a normal life. She would not have them living in a bubble.

"Well have fun and I will talk to you later." He hung up the phone. I hope she's careful, he thought. I don't know what I would do if anything happened to them.

Jason started working away at his to-do list, and was soon enveloped in the concerns of the day.

Chapter 2

Unwanted Stranger

A s she drove into the city, Maria noticed a highway warning sign flashing an Amber Alert for a lost child in the area. Great! Maria's heart went out immediately to the family of the child and she took the opportunity to cover again with her sons the "instructions": "Don't talk to strangers," "Don't go anywhere without telling me," "Don't approach anyone who asks you for help," and so on.

"You remember Donnas' little friend, Alice. She wandered away from her mother at the mall and came *that close* to being taken by a man who told her he would bring her to her mom and that her mom was outside in the parking lot. If a passerby hadn't noticed her struggling with the man and pulled her away from him, no telling what might have happened!"

"Oh, mom!" Jason said. "We aren't babies like Alice was. Besides, we're going to stick together. Right Mark?"

Mark nodded his head yes. Jason was giving him that look that told him he needed to agree with him — or suffer the consequences.

"Mark will be just fine with me," Jason said.

Maria knew that her son Jason meant every word he said but she knew that he himself was still a kid. Smiling, she looked in the mirror at her eldest son, smiled and thanked him for his concern. She was very proud of him.

"Mark, you are not to leave your brother's side. You go where he goes and you don't give him a hard time about it. Your dad and I love you boys very much. We just want you to be safe."

Jason was twelve but tall for his age. He was very protective of his younger brother and, she had observed, was much nicer to him than other boys his age were to younger siblings. Jason had even come to his brother's aid once to protect him from an older boy who was bullying him. He suffered a busted lip in the fight and got into hot water with the principle, but that bully never bothered Mark again. Jason knew from experience that his brother needed looking after. Mark was very curious and loved meeting new people.

They pulled into the parking lot just before noon and Maria was surprised to find a parking space close to a mall entryway. The mall was typically crowded and bustling, so this was a rare stroke of luck. It always made Maria nervous to bring the kids to the mall because keeping track of them in the crowd was very difficult.

Maria brought the boys with her to Sears to exchange some clothes and, predictably, the boys were both beginning to fidget. Maria knew that it was a matter of minutes before they would say they were bored so she beat them to the punch.

"Are you guys ready to go to the game room?" she asked.

They looked at their mom with faces beaming.

"YES!" they harmonized.

Maria handed Jason twenty dollars (ten for each boy) and, after he assured her that he knew exactly where the game room was, she reached out to them.

"Come on and give your mother a hug," she said.

"Aw mom, do we have to?" they harmonized again, with pained expressions.

Maria knew she was the one who needed the hug and felt her protective instincts taking over again. Though denied the hug, she recalled her commitment to get both sons outside the overprotective bubble, so she simply turned to Jason one last time.

"Remember, keep your eye on your younger brother."

"I will mom," Jason assured her.

With that, both boys turned and began walk-running to the game room.

Maria couldn't resist finding a shop close to the game room where she could covertly keep a watchful eye on the boys. Maria was able to enjoy uninterrupted shopping—aside from glancing over at the game room every one or two minutes. The boys had no idea she was watching and they were having a great time. She also noticed Jason was doing a good job keeping an eye on his brother.

Maria was able to shop for about thirty minutes and all was well with the boys. Suddenly a familiar voice caught her ear.

"Hey Maria, how's the shopping in here?"

Maria smiled as she turned. It was Janice, her next door neighbor and friend, standing there with several shopping bags dangling from her hands. It had been a week since they had last spoken; so after they hugged, they caught up.

Janice was a beautiful young lady who looked much younger than her true age (late thirties). She was a successful attorney in the Oakland area. One of Janice's clients was Bright Idea, so she had worked with Jason on a number of issues.

"Let's sit and chat for a minute. My feet are killing me," Janet said, wincing in pain.

Within minutes the two were immersed in conversation and catching up on old and new news, everything from the kids and their activities, to Bright Idea.

Maria thoroughly enjoyed talking with Janice. She was a Christian, the real deal in Maria's estimation, in that she didn't just attend church but truly was kind, loving, and had integrity (she never gossiped—very unusual). Maria always felt safe in sharing personal things with her. Janice had long tried to convince Maria and Jason to "get back into church."

Janice excused herself for a restroom break, and Maria glanced down at her watch and noted with shock that over thirty minutes had passed since she had checked on the boys. She cast a nervous glance

Love of the Father

toward the game room. She saw Jason speaking with someone there and felt a sudden stab of fear, until she realized the boy was one of Jason' school buddies. She was relieved, but only momentarily. Where was Mark?

She noticed that Jason looked upset. He and his friend were both glancing around frantically. Mark! Where was Mark? Maria wondered, a sick feeling in her stomach. God no, Mark!

Jason met her eyes and ran from the game room, in tears now.

"Mom, have you seen Mark? Where is Mark?"

Maria's fears were confirmed and she suddenly felt weak in the knees.

"I haven't seen him," she said, her voice rising, "Jason what happened?"

"He said he was tired and wanted to come out and sit with you—he could see you sitting with Miss Janice. That's the last time I saw him. I am so sorry mom," he said, voice trembling, then bursting into tears.

Maria took Jason into her arms and hugged him.

Love of the Father

"Don't worry baby—you didn't do anything wrong." She knew she had to be strong for him, though inside she felt panic rising.

"I am so sorry mom, please forgive me."

Maria looked at Jason with love and tears in her eyes.

"Jason, I love you. I am not mad at you. This is not your fault. I am sure Mark is alright and we will find him."

Jason began to calm down.

"Can you tell me anything else about your brother; when you saw him last, and where he was headed?"

Jason shook his head. He knew nothing else.

Maria controlled her panic and asked a vendor at a nearby kiosk where the security station was and that her child was lost. The vendor called security to come to them. As Maria waited for the security guard, she took out a recent picture of Mark and began asking people who passed by if they had seen her son—he was lost in the mall. After she has asked many people, one woman's face lit up when she saw the photo.

"I saw him. I saw your son!"

"Oh thank God," Maria said, choking back tears. "Where? Where did you see him?"

She turned and pointed.

"That way...about halfway through the mall," she said. "He was sitting on a bench talking with a long-haired, bearded older man. Is his grandfather with him?"

"No, his grandfather is not with him," Maria said, heart sinking.

Maria didn't wait for the security guard. She quickly followed the direction the woman had indicated, with Jason in tow. Horrible thoughts and gruesome pictures ran through her mind. Hysteria was beginning to set in. Was her worst fear becoming a reality?

Maria rounded a corner, her heart pounding in her chest. Please let him be there, she thought as her mind reeled with panic. She came within view of the bench and her mouth fell open at the view—the bench was empty. Mark was not there.

Now frantic, she began stopping more shoppers, showing them pictures of Mark. "Have you seen this boy? Have you seen my son?" No one had seen him.

It seemed Mark had vanished into thin air.

Just then, a young man walked up to Maria and said that he had seen a boy about the age of her son—and an old man was with him.

"Thank you. Thank you so much" she said. "What's your name?"

"My name is James, James Johnson."

"James, I want to be sure you saw my son. What was he wearing?"

"Sure. He had on a blue and white striped shirt, with a pair of jeans, and I think he had a pair of Under Armour shoes—I remember because I told my friend the kid had really cool shoes. If you want me to, I can take you to where I saw him."

"Oh yes, please, of course," Maria stammered.

Love of the Father

Maria and Jason followed James as he made his way quickly back to where he had seen Mark and the bearded old man. All Maria could think of as they walked was poor little Alice who had almost been snatched from this very mall. She hoped her son would also encounter a Good Samaritan. Maria wanted to know more about the man...anything more about him that James had observed. Maria asked James for anything else he could tell her.

"Well, he was tall, old, bearded, long brown and gray hair in a pony tail, and his clothes were slopped and wrinkly, like he had slept in them. And he looked a little dirty, like he hadn't taken a bath in a while. He struck me as a homeless person."

Marias heart lodged in her throat. The description seemed similar to the one of the man who tried to kidnap Alice from the mall.

"We're almost there," James said.

Just as they reached the spot, from behind her, Maria heard a sweet, familiar voice.

"Mom! Mom! What are you doing over here?"

Love of the Father

It was Mark!

Maria turned to see Mark standing before her, eyes wide with innocence, then alarm as he saw she had been crying. She immediately grabbed him up and held him close as Jason joined in. Maria looked up and saw James smiling at them. She thanked him profusely for his help. He said he was glad to help and went on his way.

"I told you to never go off with anyone!" Maria cried, her anger now rising, replacing her fear. "You NEVER speak to a stranger, much less go away with one. I don't care if they seem like the nicest person on earth—once they get you by yourself, it's too late!"

"But mom," Mark said, voice quivering, "I'm alright and if you will listen to me, I'll tell you what happened. I got tired of the arcade and thought that I would walk over to the video game store. I went the wrong direction and must have looked lost. That's when the homeless looking old man asked me if I needed help. I asked him if he knew which way I needed to go to get to the video game store.

Love of the Father

He pointed me that direction. Then he asked me if I liked Mario Cart, and I said I did and we just started talking about it, sitting on that bench over there. Isn't it weird that an old man knows about video games?"

Maria thought of about ten things she could have said during Mark's report, but held back. As they walked and Mark talked, Maria felt many eyes on them. They had caused quite a commotion. Maria was slightly embarrassed but she had no regrets. Her child had gone missing in the mall—she was going to get everyone there involved in the search if she needed to.

"Mark, don't ever do anything like that again. You had your brother and I worried to death."

"I'm sorry mom," Mark said. "I promise I will not do anything like that again."

"You do realize that I have to call your father—you know what that means, right?"

"Yes ma'am," Mark said with resignation, hanging his head.

"Mark, I can't believe you would do something this stupid," Jason added, thinking his brother was getting off easy.

"Jason, knock it off," Maria said sternly.

It was only when Maria was getting into her car that she realized she had not called Janice to let her know what had happened. She dialed Janice' number. It rang a couple times before Janice picked up.

"Hello, this is Janice!"

"Hello Janice, its Maria. I just wanted to let you know why I left you today at mall."

She told Janice the whole story, assuring her Mark was safe now and that they were driving home.

"GREAT!" Janice replied. "Did you warn him of the dangers of going off by himself? I know you must have been scared half to death."

Maria told Janice she had to end the call and call Jason. They said their goodbyes and Maria pressed Jason's number with nervous fingers for she knew how Jason reacted when he was bothered with family problems at work. Well he would just have to deal with this in his own way because this one was huge.

The phone rang several times until Deborah answered.

"Good afternoon, Bright Computers, you've reached the office of Jason Albright. How may I help you?"

"Hi Deborah, may I speak to Jason?"

"Hello Mrs. Albright! Absolutely, let me announce your call to him."

It took a few minutes for Jason to pick up the call.

"Maria, I am very busy. Is it something quick?"

Maria began recounting all that had happened and quickly became emotional. Suddenly, Jason interrupted her:

"Maria,...honey...can we continue this at home? Is there any way we can continue this at home? I have work to do?

Maria was floored.

"Well...yes, I guess," she stammered, shocked at Jason's uncaring attitude. She recovered quickly and became angry.

"I am so SORRY to have interrupted you to let you know how close we came to LOSING OUR SON!"

Jason knew he had spoken out of impatience and distraction, not indifference.

"Which son?" Jason asked—immediately realizing that this question came off wrong as well.

"WHICH SON?"

"I am sorry hon. I am glad the boys are both fine. Please have them in my study by 6:15. I'll talk to them then.

And with that, they hung up.

Maria sent the boys to the study on time, but Jason was running late, as usual. As Maria turned to leave, Mark asked her a question.

"Mom, did dad sound upset?"

"Yes and rightfully so; what you did was very dangerous. Your dad and I love you very much and losing either of you would be our worst nightmare."

Jason arrived home twenty minutes later and went straight to the study where Maria had joined the

Love of the Father

boys. He asked Maria to tell all that had happened. After about ten minutes, just after she recounted their joyful reunion, Jason nodded his head, cleared his throat, and finally interrupted Maria.

"Mark, why didn't you listen to your mother? You know better then to go off by yourself. This isn't the first time you've done something stupid like this and I am getting tired of coming home and the first thing I have to do is correct you for something," Jason said, his voice rising in anger. "Well young man, what do you have to say about all this? This had better be good."

"Dad, I left the game room to find mom but some boy just outside the game room was playing a game on his portable game player. He told me how great the game was and that I could demo it as a game store in the middle of the mall, so I went to the store to play the game."

Jason gave Mark a stern look.

"Just one minute young man. You are telling me that you left to play a game in another store — yet you were standing in a game room full of games." Jason was at a loss for words for a few seconds.

"First, you should not have left the store to go anywhere. Second, it was ridiculous to go play another game. Third, you never told your brother about this. He was put in charge of watching you. To leave him like that is like leaving your mother or me.

"Dad, I just lost track of time and, when I left the store, I couldn't find my way back. I thought I would just sit there on a bench and try to figure out how to get back or just wait there for mom to find me."

"Go on," his father prompted Mark.

"I sat there a while and then this very nice man sat down on the bench too and started talking with me. He asked if I was lost and I said I was. He sat down on the bench with me. He said, 'I promise I won't hurt you.' Then he told me that he knew our family and was a close friend of grandpa for a very long time."

"Mark, everyone around here knows us or can say they do; our name is well known. That doesn't mean you believe them or trust them. As to the man saying, 'I promise I won't hurt you,' that is what someone who may well try to hurt you would say. This is why our rule is and always has been—you don't talk to strangers."

Mark looked up at his dad and said very hesitantly, "Dad, he said something else which was kind of strange."

Both Maria and Jason braced themselves for what might follow.

"What did he say?" his father asked.

"He said that he had been trying and trying to speak to you, even whispering in your ear, and you still would not respond to him—something about a falling out a long time ago."

Maria looked at Jason quizzically. Jason just shrugged. He had no idea who this could be. He pressed Mark.

"Well Mark did this mystery man give you a name? Did he tell you where he lived? Did he leave you any other information that might help us find this man or contact him?" Boy would I love to find this guy, Jason thought.

"Umm...he did say he lives in the neighborhood and that he hoped to visit us or that we would visit him."

"Oh, my God!" Maria exclaimed, the panic beginning to rise again.

Jason was already forming an action plan.

"Mark, this stranger tells you that he knew your grandfather, that he knows me, that he and I had a falling out, AND that he lives in our neighborhood? That's it, I'm calling the police! They need to find this guy."

"Dad, please don't! He didn't do anything and besides, he seemed to be really nice," Mark pleaded.

"Well Mark, that's not good enough. There are some pretty dangerous people out there who can seem nice at first."

"But dad, he told me that something that might happen to my brother Jason and that we will need to turn to him for help." Maria, Jason, and Jason Jr. all exchanged shocked glances. "He says that once we turn to him, Jason will be fine!"

"What do you mean that something might happen to Jason? Did he say he was going to do something to Jason? Turn to him? How did he say he knew something bad would happen to Jason?"

All kinds of alarm bells were going off in Jason's mind. Maria sat in stunned silence, on the verge of tears.

Mark looked at his dad and shrugged his shoulders.

"Dad, all I know is, the man seemed to know a lot, like everything."

"Mark, a homeless, crazy man in grubby clothes sat down with you at the mall and said he knew us, and then threatened your brother. That is what happened here."

Jason paused for a moment, then looked at his son in the eye and said, "If you see this man again, I don't want you going anywhere near him. You don't

Love of the Father

say a word to him. You just let me or your mother know. Do you understand what I'm saying?"

Mark met his dad's eye, and knew he meant business. He knew better than to say anything further.

"You bet dad, that's a promise." He paused for a moment, weighed down by the thought of what he had put his parent's through.

"Mom, dad; I am really sorry."

"Mark, we just love you so much," said his mother. "I don't know what we would do if something happened to you."

"We accept your apology," said his father. "This situation is exactly why we have the rule about strangers—especially those who look like the one who sat and spoke with you."

Mark sat silently.

"Is there anything else on your mind?" his father asked.

There was something, but clearly now was not the time to share it. The man had said something else.

Mark shook his head no.

Chapter 3

A Dream

Mark went to bed with a lot on his mind that evening, not only with the day's events, but because of what the man at the mall whispered to him as he was leaving. Why would a person who seemed so nice be so immediately disliked? Was it because of his grubby clothes and unclean look? He thought about how nice the man had been and how pleasant his voice was. He hoped that this one time his father was wrong about someone. These thoughts were on Mark's mind as his eyelids grew heavy and he drifted off to sleep.

Love of the Father

It seemed like Mark had just closed his eyes when his room was filled with a blinding bright light. After a few seconds, a man walked out of the light. He looked just like the man from the mall, though dressed differently—in a long, white flowing robe. His hair glowed against the bright light and his robe billowed slightly, as if in a wind. He had sandals on his feet and a big, warm smile on his face that Mark recognized. At first Mark was frightened and tried to wake himself up, but to no avail. He sensed no danger. The closer the man came to him, the calmer Mark became. It was impossible to resist returning the man's smile.

"Mark, I heard your father talking about what happened today. You do know that he is right of course. You should not talk to strangers, regardless of how nice they seem. I know I wouldn't hurt you but there are people out there who would harm you—there is much sin in the world. Sin makes my father and I very sad. It is especially sad when one of his children falls away or separates from us. My

Love of the Father

father likes to help everyone and loves when they are happy. When people go through something bad and they blame him or me for it, it saddens us."

"Are you really Jesus, like God-Jesus, God's Son?" Mark heard himself ask. "And if you are, why did my grandma have to die?"

Mark had often heard his father express bitterness toward God over the death of his mother, Mark's grandmother. He always associated that with God.

Smiling and crouching down to Mark's level, the man said lovingly, "Mark, I am Jesus, yes. I've done no harm to your sweet grandmother. I simply took her up to heaven to be with me, my Father and with her many friends who arrived in heaven before she did, and since. She is very happy in heaven. She so longs to have your father and grandfather where she is. She wants you to know she is much happier in heaven than she was on earth and that she has always loved you very much."

Mark looked into the eyes of Jesus and asked, "Why wasn't she happy down here with all of us?"

Jesus looked at Jason and said, "She loved all of her family very, very much, but it was time for her to come here to be with us, just as all of our children will do. Where she is, she will never die. She lives. One day you will see her again, and that time will never end."

"What about Jason?" Mark asked. "You told me that he was going to be very sick or something like that. Is he going to be alright or is he going to heaven, where grandma is?"

"Well Mark, the way things turn out with Jason will be entirely up to your father."

"I don't understand—what does my father have to do with Jason being OK, or not?"

"Come with me Mark" Jesus said as he extended his hand to Mark.

Mark took Jesus' hand in his.

Instantly, Mark was walking hand in hand with Jesus in a big hallway. It seemed like a hospital hallway, like one he had seen on a TV show. There were people walking in the hallway, going about their usual business. Mark slightly brushed someone, but they didn't notice. He and Jesus seemed invisible to the people.

"Mark, I am going to let you see the future..."

A hallway and door suddenly appeared before them, a hospital. Jesus guided Mark through the door of a hospital room. He saw Jason in the bed, his eyes closed, as if sleeping. His mother, father and sister Donna were there, gathered around the bed.

"Mark, your brother Jason is going to be very sick. When that happens, your father will have an important choice to make. His choice will determine whether your brother' life will be saved or not."

Tears came to Mark's eyes as he asked, "Do you know what choice my dad will make? My brother makes me mad sometimes, but he is a good brother and I do love him very much. I don't want anything bad to happen to him."

Jesus sat down in front of Mark, gently took his hand and said, "Mark, my Father and I love you and your family very much. We know how much you love your family. We love you so much that we will go to great lengths to make sure you never die but that someday you will join us in heaven. We've chosen you to lead your family back to us."

Mark began to cry and looked up into Jesus' eyes.

"I am just a kid. How can I help? Wouldn't it be better for you to go to my father so he can do it?"

Jesus looked at Mark tenderly and said, "We've been trying to reach your father for a long time. So far he has refused to open his heart to us. We accomplish some of our greatest wonders and miracles through children. We will reach your family through your heart that is tender toward us and your brother's suffering."

"I don't understand" Mark said, sobbing. "I just don't understand this."

"Step by step you will understand. You have much to learn, much to do, and have very little time. I have to take you on a special trip."

Jesus gripped Mark's hand again.

"Where are we going?" Mark asked?

Love of the Father

"I am going to show you my Father's house and let you see your grandmother so it will be planted in your mind and in your heart. You will need to see this to be able to lead your family back to me," Jesus said.

In what seemed only a blink of his eye, Mark was walking hand in hand with Jesus on the streets of a place filled with songs of praise to God and joy. Angels moved through the air, worshipping God. Everything was snow white. It seemed every person he saw was smiling and singing praises to the Lord. There was no anger or sadness, just joy and happiness. The gates were made of gold that shined brightly; like the sun. There were no cars, no stores that sold groceries or clothes. Everyone was peaceful and joyful. Their garments were white, with gold trimmings.

"Where are we?" Mark asked.

"You're getting a glimpse of heaven Mark. This is very special. Only a few people who still live life on earth have seen this. I want you to see someone who is very special to you. I want her to tell you in her words how she is doing here."

Mark walked with Jesus on a street of gold. Everything around them glistened in the light.

After walking a short distance, Jesus said to Mark, "This is the place. The person waiting for you is behind the door, straight ahead."

"It's my grandma, isn't it?" Mark asked with a smile spreading across his face.

Jesus simply smiled back.

As Mark took the last few steps to the door, tears began to roll down his cheeks. His knees trembled as he stood before the door. He opened it slowly and walked into a beautiful room full of flowers. The scents were amazing! He smelled roses, lilac, and lavender. (It reminded him of grandma's earthly flower garden, but this was far more beautiful.)

Sounds of trumpets and harps met his ear and Mark could hear the voice of a woman singing, "Glory to God in the highest and peace to His people on earth!"

As Mark walked further, he noticed a woman standing at a window, dressed in a white gown with gold trim. She began walking toward him. As she approached, Mark recognized her—it was in fact his grandmother, though not frail as he had last seen her, but youthful, as he had seen in her photo albums. Mark was overwhelmed by the fact that his grandma had died and was now alive and standing before him!

As she drew up to him, he saw that her face glowed, and light radiated from within her. Her white hair flowed gently down past her shoulders. Her face was peaceful and kind. She looked so happy. Mark thought that she must have gone through a lot on earth because she never looked like this.

"Grandma!" Mark shouted, "I miss you so much!" He ran to meet her. They met in the middle of the room, his grandma kneeling down so she could wrap her arms around Mark. She held him close.

She whispered in Mark's ear, "My dear little Mark, I love you so much and can scarcely wait until the time comes when we can all be together again!"

"Grandma, is this really heaven?

"Yes Mark, it really is heaven. Isn't it beautiful? You've never felt so much peace and love in a place until you come here. There is no hatred or meanness here, just peace, harmony, and love. Jesus has brought you here so that you can lead your mom and dad back to the Father. Jesus knows that after you have seen and experienced this, your parents will listen and believe!"

"Grandma, how will I be able to help—I'm just a kid? I can't make mom and dad go to church and besides, dad said that he doesn't want God talked about in his house. That's what he said the last time I asked to go to church with my friend, Darren."

A tear rolled down Mark's cheek as he said this. His grandmother hugged him close again, comforting him.

"My son, your father was a bit tough. I truly hoped I would be able to help him find his way, but I ran out of time—and he wasn't ready then."

Love of the Father

"Let me tell you a little bit about your father," his grandma said as she sat down with him in the middle of the floor. "Before you were born, your dad was very close to God. He went to church all the time. Even as a youth, your father would begin each day with prayer and thanksgiving, asking God to show him how he could serve him better. He even gave money to charities—especially to those that helped children who were hungry and needy. He actually followed Christ then."

"I've never seen him pray or give thanks to God. What happened? He won't even let my friend Darren take me to church. Why doesn't he even let us talk about God in our house?

"When your father's business began failing, at first he prayed and prayed, believing that God would turn things around. Your father thought God had turned his back on him. He stopped praying. When I left the earth to come here to be with Jesus, your father started using that as an excuse for not worshipping the Father and for not speaking to Jesus."

Love of the Father

Mark looked at his grandma with a puzzled look on his face.

"I don't understand. I don't know much about business, but my friend Darren says that God gives us choices but it is up to us to make the right ones."

"Darren is absolutely correct Mark," his grandmother replied. "Jesus allows things to happen for the purpose of seeing how strong our faith in Him is. When bad things happen, will we draw closer to God, or step away from Him? We all have this choice. I know you are too young to really understand this, but you will one day. Your father, when his prayer was not answered as he hoped, chose to step away from God."

Mark heard someone calling to him—as if from inside him, though His grandma heard it as well.

"Mark, it's time for you to go. I wish we had more time but this is the way of it for now. Let your family know how much I love them, and for them to have faith in God so that I will see them again."

Mark looked at his grandmother, then toward the voice that was calling him and said, voice trembling: "Grandma do I have to go? I miss you so much and I don't want to leave you. Can you at least ask Jesus to let me stay a while longer?"

He hugged his grandmother tightly after saying this, knowing he would not be allowed to stay.

"Precious Mark." his grandmother said as she held him. "It isn't your time yet and you have work to do on earth. I know that when your time comes I will see you again."

They hugged one last time before Mark turned and stepped away.

"I love you Mark," his grandmother said.

"I love you too Grandma and I promise to be good so I can come up here and stay!"

Walking out of the house, Mark noticed that angels were everywhere and they were singing praises to God. Then out of the cloud walked his friend, Jesus.

Love of the Father

"Mark, it is time for you to return home. When you wake up tomorrow, you will first think that this was all a dream. Soon after you will know that it was not."

Jesus knelt down and said, "Mark, your brother will become gravely ill. He must not fear, nor should you. What you have seen and heard here will come back to you. You will share this dream with your mother and father, that you went to heaven and saw Grandma there, and that she was very happy."

Mark still didn't know a lot about God the Father, or Jesus, but after speaking with his grandma, and Jesus, he knew that they were absolutely loving and kind—that his father was wrong not to see them that way. But he also knew that his dad had experienced a lot of pain which might be keeping him from seeing Jesus for who He is.

When Mark woke up the next morning he could hardly wait to tell his family about the dream. The breakfast table was quieter than usual, until Mark said he had a dream about grandma the night before.

The family sat in stunned silence until Maria gently queried her youngest son, "Mark, honey, what do you mean? What kind of dream?"

"I dreamed that I was floating on a cloud and I went to heaven. There was a lot of singing for God, and there were angels flying all around. There was a small house there and grandma lived in it and had a huge flower garden. She was smiling and singing with the angels."

"Oh, really?" his father said. "I guess the next thing you will tell me is that Jesus was there."

"Yes, there was that man named Jesus, but I don't remember much about him. All I remember was that he seemed like a real nice man and that he is taking good care of grandma."

Mark's brother Jason looked at him, slightly peeved.

"So Mark, did you ask this Jesus person why he took our grandmother from us and why did He not answer dad when his business was having problems? People say Jesus loves us, but if he does, why does he let bad things happen to us?"

"Grandma said that you would probably make fun and not believe, but it would be alright," Mark said. Mark knew that he was not telling the whole truth when he said that but he had to convince them somehow.

"Everything was real! Grandma said to tell you that she loves each of you and wants you to have faith in God so you can be with her again one day."

His father had heard enough. He stood up quickly saying, "Mark, that's it. Not a word more."

He shook his head, turned on his heel and left the room as the family sat in stunned silence.

Chapter 4

Reflection

As Jason walked to his car to leave for work, all he could think about was Mark's outrageous dream and the nonsense about Jesus and his dear mom—making miss her badly once again. So many times he had told his family that he did not want Jesus discussed in his home, yet *still* they bring Him up!

He got into his car and paused for a moment, thinking about his religious "history." Yes business went bad and he wondered why God didn't step in and rescue him quickly. Yes his mother had died earlier than she should have and that caused a crisis. But there was more to it.

Things started well enough at Bright Idea and they enjoyed outstanding success—at first. Anything and everything they touched seemed to turn into money. They were flush with cash and living large.

Then seven years ago they began to see a decline in sales, followed by a dive in profits. Suddenly, nothing they did seemed to work. While they were enjoying the money and short work days, hungry competitors had entered the market—their products were just better. They had fallen asleep at the wheel.

They did everything in their power to keep clients—begging them to stay and promising that exciting products would be coming soon. Their desperate efforts worked and they kept enough clients to stay afloat. However, for them to see the light at the end of the tunnel, they needed to sign one more sizable client.

Love of the Father

He prayed and prayed for God to intervene and make a difference in their business. After a few days, and seeing no change in the circumstances, Jason decided God was not listening or did not care, so his prayers became occasional. God helps those who help themselves, Jason concluded.

The best idea Jason could think of was to raise prices and cut costs by lowering quality standards for their computer parts. He hyped up his marketing, describing Bright Idea computers, business systems, and custom software "new and improved." Before long, Bright Idea was back "on top" and in good shape. It was short-lived.

Soon after, the cheap computer parts caught up with them—customer complaints skyrocketed and their reputation was on the rocks. There were allegations of theft of intellectual property in some of their new custom business software. (This was actually true, but ultimately could not be proven, so Bright Idea dodged a bullet.) The business went into decline again.

Jason still prayed occasionally for the business but could not understand why God was not helping them—if God was real at all. After all, they had lived their lives as Christians, had attended church, had given money in the offering, so where was God when they needed Him?

As business went from bad to horrible, Jason felt that God had abandoned him. He turned his back on God. He stopped attending church and forbid his wife from attending. When Maria questioned his decision, she was not satisfied.

"Have you tried prayer?" Maria asked.

"I have," Jason responded, but either he doesn't hear me, he doesn't care to help me, or he's not there.

"Honey, I understand your disappointment, but that is not the way to look at this. God has helped us every other time we've been in need, so if we keep standing together in faith, I am sure that things will get better—"

"No way; no more waiting around. I'm done. I'll do what needs to be done for the business to succeed. I understand it's up to me." Then he turned and walked away.

"I cannot believe that you have let this business carry you down to a level of the 'no-good's' that hang out on the street corner trying to take advantage of those that don't know any better. You may as well put a gun to your client's heads and make them buy your stuff, like an armed robber, because to God what you are doing is the same thing."

Jason turned and walked back to where she was standing and pointing his finger in her face, shouting, "Don't ever raise your voice to me! I told you about saying 'God' in this household. I FORBID IT!" With a final glare, he turned and walked away.

Maria knew that her husband could get violent when he lost his temper so she decided to do as he asked for now. She knew that this was not the right thing to do. Perhaps if she had been a little stronger and stood her ground, he may have backed off a little. She did not like the idea of getting away from the church and especially God.

Love of the Father

Bringing up her children without any Christian influence was a disturbing thought for her. The thought of the failure of the business gave Maria a sick feeling in the pit of her stomach (after all, they had one child already and another on the way). She decided to continue her personal prayer time and asking God for His divine help in getting Jason to change his direction and to repent of the things he had done and intended to do. Maria loved being in contact with God and hoped that He did not hold this against her.

After Jason calmed down, Maria would approach him again and talk with him. One thing she knew that she would have to do is make sure that what she was doing would not get out—that meant not telling the children.

Jason went directly to the office to meet his father to discuss their ideas for saving the business. It was rare for them to have a Saturday meeting, but under the circumstances, necessary.

Love of the Father

Jason's father arrived a little bit after Jason and they immediately sat down and started going through the paperwork. They had not gone very far when they both realized that there was no way that they could keep the business afloat. They needed a bold new plan and both were committed to do whatever was required to save the business.

"Well son we have no choice. Either we cut expenses, find new business, or we go bottom up."

"How in the world do we cut expenses? We've cut them to the bone!"

"I know some people who can solve our problem. By using the products they supply,, and by using products they supply, we would cut our expenses by fifty percent."

Jason let out a long whistle, as he let that thought sink in, but then the full weight of what his father suggested hit him.

"But dad, the only way we can cut costs that deeply is if the products we sell are low grade, or... stolen,"

"Well son, we are out of choices. We either do what we've done and lose everything, or we take a chance with this to save our company. Who knows? Our profit could be in the *millions!*"

Jason pondered this for a moment. His father had never suggested anything like this before. Jason had already tried the low budget parts route—there were no other choices on the table. What would his mother have said, good Christian woman that she was? She would have nipped it in the bud—he had no doubt of this.

Then the other side of Jason's brain took over. Businesses do this all the time. Most of our competitors probably do this. Anything is better than losing the company. Still, a sudden pang of conscience made him questions his father one last time.

"Dad, how do you think God looks at this?"

"Now you are sounding like your mother. What in the world does God have to with this? This is business. Besides, we've already tried that, praying and all. It didn't work. Must be one of those times when he wants us to help ourselves. Oh, and by the way—this is not something to discuss with your mother."

"Suppose mom finds out? She has ways of finding out stuff like this."

"If she says anything to me, I will tell her point blank that we had no choice but to do what we had to do to save the business. We tried prayer and sought God, but He evidently did not want to help us, so we sought another way to make the business work so skipped the prayer and God stuff and did what we needed to do.

"I don't know dad we have been so close to God all these years and now when times get tough we are bailing out on Him? It is like we are not giving Him a chance. To think like this makes me feel bad or that I am letting Him down somehow."

Mr. Albright looked at his son directly in the eye and said, "Well son, you can either choose living on the street and raising your kids on the street and go with God, or you can choose to follow my way and stay living where you are living. As for me, I am going the way I want, and since I own the biggest part of the company, that leaves you no choice."

So it had come to this. Now his father was threatening to kick him out of the company.

"I guess you give me no choice," Jason said to his father. "I just hope you know what you're doing."

That was the last time that Jason talked to his father about the whole situation and he promised his dad that he would go along with the idea, look the other way, and allow his father to strike the deal that would help the company get back on track. With that, his father struck a deal with the inexpensive "supplier" and struck his "deal with the devil."

Jason hadn't been honest with his family about why he left the church. It was all the lying, cheating and dirty dealing that he did with the business. For Jason, thinking of Jesus just reminded him of how many wrong turns he had taken. All he felt was bad when he thought of Jesus. How could he ever live up to Jesus' standards? He couldn't and nobody else

Love of the Father

could either. When he stopped thinking of Jesus, he felt better. This was the real reason Jason had given up on church and allowing any Jesus or God discussions in their home.

As business picked up, Jason's father was convinced that he had made the right decision. Jason had to admit, it all seemed to be working. Not long after he and his father turned the business around, Maria became pregnant with their third child.

It was now seven years later. Business was booming and the bank account was overflowing. The family was growing. Everyone was happy. What more could a father ask for?

Chapter 5

Mark Goes to Church

Mark was throwing a ball in the yard with his friend David, waiting for his dad to get home from work. He decided to ask David a question he had been puzzling over ever since his dream. Looking at David with a grin, he asked, "Have you ever heard of Jesus before?"

"Huh?" David said as he walked, ball in hand, to where Mark stood. "Have you ever heard of Jesus before? I think everybody has heard of Jesus. He died on the cross for our sins. If he hadn't we would all go to hell when we die—a place of fire and torture and pain. Why are you asking? Didn't you know that about Jesus?"

Mark looked at David and just shook his head no. He was a little shocked with what he just heard about hell. Mark recounted the complete dream for David, as he told him how Jesus took him to heaven and allowed him to visit with his grandmother.

David looked at as if in shock. Jesus brought you to heaven and took you to see your grandmother, David said in a high and excited pitched voice. Awesome he said, totally awesome. How was it? Was it pretty and did you see any angels?

Mark told David that his dad would not allow them to talk about Jesus in the house for some reason that he doesn't know of. Mark told David that he heard the angels singing and praying to God.

"Man, I don't know what is wrong with your dad because Jesus did a lot of good things while he was on earth. I read about him in one of our books at school. Did you know that Jesus healed a blind man so he regained his sight? He also healed a crippled man who could not walk. You know what else he did?"

David seemed really excited about miracles Jesus had done. And Mark was overcome by it all—he was hearing it all for the first time. He smiled at his friend.

"No David, I don't know but I am sure you will tell me."

"A friend of his named Lazarus died...and Jesus raised him from the dead—back to life!"

"Now I find that hard to believe. I am going to ask him about that when I see him again."

"Wouldn't it be awesome if Jesus would come down and bring my grandpa and your grandma back to life?"

"To tell you the truth, my grandmother seemed really happy where she was...I am not sure she would want to come back. Maybe your grandfather is way happier there too."

"I hadn't thought about that," David answered with his head hung down. Boy did he wish Jesus would take him to heaven to visit his grandpa. Then he dove in, explaining a few things he knew about God and Jesus.

"Okay, God is Jesus' dad, and then there is the Holy Spirit. All three are one—God. God put Jesus on earth in human form so He could teach us about God and how we could get to heaven. Mary was the woman that was chosen to give birth to Jesus as a human baby because she lived a good life and loved God. Mary's husband was upset when he found out she was going to have a baby, but God sent an angel to talk to him and then he wasn't mad anymore."

Mark interrupted David, "So Jesus had a stepdad named Joseph?

David said, "Well kinda'...yeah, I guess you can say that."

"Wow, I've never heard any of this before."

"You're kidding! How does your family celebrate Christmas? Jesus is the whole reason for Christmas—it is a celebration of Jesus' birth."

"All we do at Christmas is buy each other lots of gifts, eat a lot of food, and have people over. I wonder if my mom or dad knows this. Let's go inside and ask my mom."

The boys ran into the house. Mark found his mother in the kitchen.

"Mom, can I ask you a question—and will you promise that you won't get mad?"

Maria chuckled, "I promise that I will not get mad; ask away."

"Well David was just telling me about Christmas and what it really means, about Jesus being born, and that his mother's name was Mary. He says that Jesus' birth is the reason we celebrate Christmas. Why haven't I heard this story before? Then he said that Jesus died on a cross for our sins and that if hadn't, we would all have to go to hell!"

Maria was not expecting this type of question, so was caught a little of guard. After the dream he shared, she could understand him asking some questions.

"Where is Jason when you need him," she said under her breath.

"Sit down next to me," she told Mark. David stood nearby.

David looked at Maria and said, "When we ask my mom questions about God, she always prays first, because she never knows what we'll ask!"

This caused Maria to laugh. She could relate.

Mark asked, "Mom why don't we ever go to church like David does?"

She was a little uncomfortable answering in front of David, but did so anyway.

"Well Mark, it is really a choice me and your father made some time ago. You've never shown an interest before now. It's just not something our family does or is going to do. To believe in Jesus, that He died on the cross for your sins and loving one another the way He said to is more important than going to church. I don't believe that one is sent to hell for not going to church, but for doing something that is against God, like killing someone, stealing or purposely hurting others."

Maria stopped when it seemed that that the boys were "unmoved" by her answer. She continued with a more conciliatory tone.

"But it is nice that David's family goes to church. One day perhaps we may go, but I am not promising."

"But mom, I never heard of Him so how do I know what to do?" Mark asked.

Maria was tired of this rule in their home. She was suddenly struck with how wrong it was to deny a child the truth about God.

"I am so sorry Mark. I will do what I can to help your father to see the need to change this rule. Dear, dear Mark, I love you so much and all I want for you is the best. It's just—"

Just then, a timer went off and Maria had to tend to some baking.

Mark thought about what she said and was saddened by it. He had to get his family to church.

David sidled up to him and whispered, "Mark, if you really want to go to church, there is a way you can go. I'll just ask my mom and dad if you can watch a movie with us Saturday and then you can stay overnight. Then you can go with us to church on Sunday morning."

Mark loved the idea. "I'll ask my mom."

As his mother walked back into the room, Mark asked, "Mom, David and his family are going to a movie Saturday night, and he wants me to go and then stay the night. Please mom, can I please?"

"That sounds fine to me, just as long as you obey David's parents just as you do us."

"I will mom, I promise."

"Cool!" said David.

With that, the boys tumbled out into the yard to hash out their plans for Saturday night as they waited for Mark's dad to get home.

Saturday came, and Mark went to the movies with David and his family. Though Mark loved the movies, he was most excited about going to church and finding out more about Jesus.

Sunday morning came and everyone dressed for church. On the way there, Mark happened to mention that he had never been to church in his whole life, not as far back as he could remember.

Mrs. Morgan, David's mom, was incredulous.

"Why in the world is that? Don't your parents go to church?"

"We've never gone. My mom said that they just decided a long time ago not to go to church. But a few days ago, I had this really cool dream where I went to heaven with Jesus. I saw my grandmother there. But when I tried to tell my family about it, my dad said he didn't want to hear about it. I guess I upset him somehow. But after meeting Jesus and learning some things about Him in my dream, I want to know more about Him."

Mrs. Morgan was troubled when she heard that Mark's family didn't go to church, but seemed pleased when she heard of Mark's dream.

"That sounds like some dream! It's so good to have you with us. Well, we are taking you to what is called a catholic church, St. Michael the Archangel Catholic Church. We really like the priest at this church. His name is Michael; we call him Father Michael. We will try to introduce you after church. Oh, by the way, there is some standing, kneeling and sitting done at various times during the service, or mass, so just do what David does."

Mark had no idea what she was talking about but tried to make the best of it. He asked innocently, "Will I see Jesus there?"

David's family laughed, which surprised Mark.

Mrs. Morgan noticed that Mark looked confused.

"I am sorry Mark. That was a good question. We would love to see Jesus at church, in human form, but we don't. We do learn about him and pray to Him. As we pray together, we believe our prayers reach heaven and that Jesus answers each and every one of them.

Mark looked at David with a funny look on his face.

"How can you believe in someone you can't see? I know that Jesus exists because I have seen him. If I hadn't, it would be very hard for me to believe."

David jumped into the conversation.

"Mom prays to Jesus for things and asks him for certain favors—and she says he gives them to her. Mom always said that if we run into any problems, to always turn to him and ask him for help. If we believe he will help, he will."

"I can see why your mom would believe then, but why do you believe, David?"

"Well for one thing, back before I met you, I got really sick one time and was in the hospital. My mom called for Father O'Brien to come and say a prayer over me. When Father O'Brien got there, he spoke with my mom and dad and the doctor for quite a while. I knew something was seriously wrong with me. Father finally came in and said a long prayer. After he prayed, he said everything was going to be alright. I asked him if I was going to go to heaven. He said not yet. But I was so scared that I asked Jesus for help. If he made me well, I would be good! A few days later I began feeling better. In a week I was well

Love of the Father

enough to go home. That is just one reason why I believe in Jesus, and always will."

There was not much conversation after that because they were pulling into the church parking lot. Once in the parking lot Mark took note of all the figurines and statues stood out in front of the church

"What are all those statues?" Mark asked.

David responded, "Remember Jesus dying for our sins? That's how He did it—He died on a cross. The others are of different people who are considered saints by the church. I learn about them every day in school."

Mark was not clear about the saints and all, but mulled over what David said. He followed David's family into church. There was a huge crowd of people there. He quietly slid quietly into the pew next to his friend and remembered to keep an eye on David, to do what he did.

As the organ rang out, everyone stood to sing. After following David through all the actions and things to say, they reached the part David called the "homily." This was the time when the priest stood and talked for several minutes about what Jesus expects people to do. Mark was very tuned in to this part of the service, when suddenly the voice of Jesus, from the mall, and from his dream, spoke to him.

"Mark, I am so glad to have you here amongst my people. You have pleased my Father very much and He is very pleased with you. I will come to you again tonight, for there is a lot of work to do with your family in order for them to enter heaven. Remember, it will be your father's choice if your brother lives through his sickness or dies from it. Now close your eyes and ask for God to forgive you of your sins and to give you strength to do what I want you to do."

Mark did as Jesus told him, thinking about Jesus dying for him, and of the crucifixion statue he had seen when entering the church. When he had finished, he opened his eyes. He looked around and noticed that the people sitting around him were all staring at him. "Did I do something wrong?" he asked.

David smiled, "No, it was just those funny little noises you were making when you had your eyes shut."

"Jesus was speaking to me and I was talking to him," Mark said. "He told me to say a prayer of forgiveness and one for strength so I can help my parents."

Mark caught Mrs. Morgan's eye.

"Mrs. Morgan, is it possible for me to talk to Jesus? I mean, I didn't really know who He was until He came to me in my dream."

Mrs. Morgan smiled, "Mark, although you may not have known Him, Jesus knew you, even when you were being formed in your mother. He knows each and every one of us and loves every one of us, even before we know him. His Father created each of us with a heart to love him. He also gave us the freedom to choose to love him and pray to him or not to. Either way, he loves us. God also forgives us for any sin that we may commit if we just turn to him, ask his forgiveness and for strength to resist that sin in the future."

Mrs. Morgan could tell that by the blank look on Mark's face that she had overwhelmed him a bit.

"I'll tell you what Mark. I will invite the priest from our church over to dinner sometime soon. The next time we do, we'll invite you—and your parents if they'd like."

"Thanks!" Mark said. "You know what I am having trouble with, Mrs. Morgan? If Jesus is so good, why doesn't everybody love Him?"

"Mark, remember when I told you that God gives us choices in our life to love him or not? He has done this for our family and yours. We understood that and our family has chosen to love God, to live our lives for him. He knows that your family has chosen the opposite, but He hasn't given up. In spite of your father choosing not to speak of Jesus or God, which does hurt God, He loves your family very much."

"I guess I will understand it all one day," Mark said as they drove up in his driveway. Mark thanked the Morgan's for bringing him to church and for the movie.

"Mark, it was good to have you with us this morning," Mrs. Morgan said. "I'll be sure to let you know when we have Father O'Brien over for dinner so you and perhaps your mother or father can join us."

"Thank you!" Mark said.

As Mark walked into his home, he was greeted by his older brother Jason who promptly put him in a headlock and mussed his hair.

"Quit it!" Mark exclaimed, irritated.

He went looking for his parents and found them in the den. He walked in.

His mother's eyes brightened when she saw him. "Did you have a good time? We missed you."

"Sure did! I learned all about Jesus and how he died for our sins and how he was crucified on the cross. Just then, Mark turned to his dad, slightly panicked for breaking the rule on mentioning Jesus at home.

Love of the Father

His dad acted like he never heard him—then got up and left the room.

The rest of the day was spent with the usual laid-back Sunday activities of hanging around the house and watching television. The family ate dinner around 7 p.m. and by the time everything was said and done, it was going on 8 p.m. and almost time for bed. Mark excused himself and went up to bed.

His parents thought it odd that Mark, who usually begged to stay up late, was hitting the sack early. After hugging his mom, Mark headed upstairs to get go to bed.

As Mark put on his pajamas, he remembered what Jesus had told him earlier,"Tonight I will come to you again."

Chapter 6

A Second Warning

As Mark lay in his bed, he was not nervous about Jesus coming to see him, he was excited. Again and again he tossed over in his mind all he had learned and experienced that day at church. His mind turned to the statues he had seen outside the church.

He focused on the statue depicting the crucifixion of Christ, the one with Jesus on the cross. "He died for our sins," David had said. This Jesus must be a pretty super guy if he was willing to give up his life for us, Mark thought, I wonder why he was killed in the first place? He thought about what he had heard in church about Jesus telling us to love one another, to help the poor, and things like that. So why would anyone want to nail Jesus to a cross?

He remembered what Jesus told him in church, telling Mark to pray for forgiveness from his sins and for strength. He recalled Jesus saying he would visit him again tonight. Mark closed his eyes and soon felt himself relaxing into sleep. He began to dream. First he had a bad dream about his brother Jason in the hospital. This woke him up, but after drinking a glass of water, he returned to his bed and fell asleep again. He began to dream again.

Mark saw a bright light coming toward him. After several seconds, he could make out a figure walking toward him in the light. It was a woman and she was dressed in a golden gown. On her head, or just atop her head was a circle that shined brightly. The woman was beautiful and she had such a kind, loving expression on her face. He felt love and warmth. He felt safe.

The woman spoke, "Mark, I am Mary, the mother of Jesus. I know your name because my son has sent me to receive you and to bring you to him. Mark, my son and his Father love you very much. They love your family as well. They want you and your whole family to spend eternity with your grandmother. It will be totally up to them, for everyone has a free will. The choice set before every person is eternity in heaven or eternity in hell.

"It is entirely up to each person, how to live their either to love God with all their heart or to live their life without God in it. Following God is very hard and takes a lot of work. Some people are not willing to put forth the effort required to follow him. God expects all of his people to love and help others and not to steal, kill, or talk ugly about others. Sometimes you have to do something that you don't quite know why you have to.

"The Father knows that you are very young and realizes that this is a lot to lay on you at one time but he believes in you and knows that you will do whatever he asks."

This was a lot for Mark to take in and understand.

"You must convince your father to turn to God and accept Him if he wants his son to live. Your father will have to choose between his love for money and love for God. Your father, by inviting God back into his life, will save your brother."

Mark felt his body begin to rise into the air. Soon he could see clouds and then he was passing through them. He could hear the sound of angels singing and harps playing and saw the great gates to heaven that shined so bright.

Mary guided him into a large room. In the room stood Jesus, smiling and motioning for Mark to go to Him.

"Come here my son," Jesus said, holding out his hand to Mark.

Mark took Jesus' hand and they began walking back down a long hallway that separated some of the rooms. There were many doors down this hallway. When Mark had asked Mary why there were so many rooms, she told him that these contained the names of people that were coming before the father in a short time.

"My Father was pleased to see you in church," Jesus said. "Your tender heart, your request for forgiveness of sin, and your prayer for strength to be God's messenger to your family have all touched the Father's heart."

Mark felt joy at hearing this. This emboldened him to ask some burning questions.

"How can I help God—I am just ten years old? How will I be able to get my dad to listen to me? What do I do?"

"Mark," Jesus said, "the Father lost your dad several years ago when he and your grandfather walked away from him due to their business difficulties and the death of your grandmother. They thought the Father had let them down. But he was merely testing them and their faith. Had they kept their faith in him even just a little bit longer, they would have received peace over the death of your grandmother and their business would have been restored. They gave up on God. You can help lead your father back to God and save your brother Jason."

"I've never been able to convince my father to do anything before."

"Mark, God wants your dad back and he will do anything to win back his soul. It will be your father's choice whether to spend eternity with us here in heaven or to spend eternity in hell. The choice he makes will also determine if your brother comes to heaven sooner, dying from a mysterious disease, or if he pulls through and lives a long, happy life. All of this depends on the choice your father makes."

"I promise I will do my best to help my dad turn back to Jesus and to save my brother," Mark said.

Jesus smiled

"I know you will Mark, I know you will. Not only will you be a part of bringing your dad back to worshiping me, but it will also save your brother's life."

Mark was feeling overwhelmed by the responsibility he carried but he believed what Jesus said. He suddenly gained confidence.

"I am sure my dad will do what he must do to save his own soul as well as my brother's life," Mark said.

Love of the Father

"Remember this Mark, it is not simply a matter of your father saying a prayer. It's more complicated than that. The real test for your father will be whether or not he is willing to give up the things in his life that he loves more than me and that he means the words of the prayer. In this way he will assure my Father that he has truly changed, and that he is willing to put others before himself, ahead of cars, boats, or a big house."

"So my dad will have to give up our house, our cars, and all the other stuff we have? Will we have no place to live? No way to get around?"

Jesus sat down and placed Mark on his lap.

In a voice that would quiet the angels, he said, "Mark my dear son, I cannot answer that for the Father, for only he knows the answer. I can promise you that if your dad makes the right choice; your family will be blessed beyond your wildest dreams. What I can say is that anything your father gives will be returned to him and more."

Mark wondered about being blessed beyond his wildest dreams. That and heaven sounded good to him.

"When will I know to do these things that you want me to do in order to save my father and brother?"

"I will be with you the whole time, even when you cannot see me. I will hold your hand and guide you," Jesus assured him. "You must go now Mark. Remember that God loves you and your family very much and he is willing to help them spend eternity in heaven—a place where there is pure love, peace, harmony, no worries, and no problems."

Mark turned to find Mary, Jesus' mother waiting for him. She extended her hand to Mark and he walked over to her. She hugged Mark tightly just as she had held Jesus when he was a baby. It seemed only a second later that Mark woke up lying in his bed. Man, what a dream! His first thought was, I dare not tell my father about this! He closed his eyes again and drifted off into a deep, restful sleep. The next thing he heard was his mother's morning call to breakfast.

When Mark opened his eyes that morning he remembered the dream he had and what Jesus had told him about his dad and what Jason would go through. The confidence he had the previous night was gone and he feared that he was incapable of getting his father to the point where he would pray the simple prayer. But then he remembered that Jesus had assured him that he would be with him, watching over him. He felt the confidence rise again.

Mark was last to join the family at the breakfast table. His mother did not seem to mind this morning. He walked over to her and gave her a big hug and a kiss. Then he walked over and gave his dad the same.

"Well someone certainly woke up on the right side of the bed this morning," his mother smiled.

"Good morning Mark."

"Morning," Mark returned.

"So Mark," his father began, "you never told us how it went over at David's house this past weekend. Did you boys have fun? What did you do?"

Mark didn't want to mention going to church first because he knew what would happen if he did.

"We had an amazing time. We went to the mall, saw a movie, played games and went out to eat. Maybe our family should do that soon too, you know?"

Mark knew what was next and he hoped he would be able to cover it up.

No sooner had he thought about it then his dad turned to him and asked, "So what did you do on Sunday morning? I know that David's parents go to church. Did you go with them?"

"No," Mark lied. "David and I stayed home with his dad while his mom went."

"Good," his brother Jason interjected, "because I don't want to get into the 'no talking about Jesus,' and 'no going to church' thing."

Everyone seemed willing to drop the conversation there.

Mark took a deep breath and sighed with relief. He knew he had lied his way out of a situation that could have been bad. He sure hoped that Jesus would forgive him for lying.

After breakfast, Mark found his mother alone in the kitchen. He wanted to tell her everything.

"Mom, I had a bad dream last night that woke me up," Mark said.

"Oh really," his mother responded. "Tell me about it." His mom always had time to talk, it seemed. Mark loved that about her.

"Well it started out that we were all in the hospital because Jason was very sick. The doctor was in Jason's room, just looking at him. Suddenly I found myself all alone. You and dad were gone, so I started looking for you. I was walking down a long hallway that was full of doctors and nurses. I asked everyone where you or dad had gone, but nobody seemed to know. The next thing I was back in Jason's room and you were both there. You were both crying and arguing. You were trying to get dad to pray for Jason but dad was telling you he wouldn't pray because he didn't believe in it. You told him he was being stubborn and hard-headed, that Jason's life was on the line and that no matter what, you were going to the chapel to pray, with or without him. With tears in your eyes you left the room and left dad with Jason."

"That does sound scary."

"It looked so real and I could see the tubes all over him and I could hear the doctors telling you and dad that they had done as much as they could; that it was in God's hands now. You know mom I heard the doctors tell you and dad this but I wasn't worried at all because I knew God would help dad make the right choice."

His mother had a tear in her eye.

"I remembered that Jesus and His Father are looking over us, and as long as they are there, Jason will be alright."

"You are absolutely right. We have nothing to worry about." She gave him a big hug.

Chapter 7

A Son's Sickness, a Father's Test

Mark had a great day after sharing his dream with his mother. The emotional drama of the dream and the weight he felt from carrying the responsibility to lead his father back to Jesus had been heavy. After talking with his mother, the weight had lifted.It also reassured him of his parent's love for him, his brother, and sister. He would rest well that evening, knowing Jesus would help him. He hoped his mom would keep up her end and say a prayer for dad.

The rest of the day was uneventful.

That evening the family turned in for the night at the usual time. Little did they know that this would be the calm before the storm. It seemed Jason's head had barely hit his pillow when he was awakened by his brother Jason crying out for his mother. A shiver of fear went up Mark's back; Jason was sick.

"Is Jason okay mom?" Mark called out.

"He's fine. It's okay, just go back to bed," she answered.

No sooner had Mark returned to his bed and gotten comfortable, when his mother's scream made him sit straight up in his bed. He bolted to Jason's room. She was holding Jason, who was limp in her arms. His father had reached the room just before him.

"He's unconscious and he has a high fever!" his mother cried out. "Call 9-1-1!"

As his father dialed 9-1-1, and his mother tended to Jason, all Mark could think to do is call out silently to Jesus.

Within a minute, they heard the sirens as the ambulance pulled onto their street, then into their driveway. Mark ran with his father to the front door to let the two paramedics in. They moved rapidly to Jason's room and went to work checking his vital signs, trying to discern his condition. Mark was amazed at how quickly they worked.

One of the paramedics began asking his mom questions.

"How old is the young man?"

"Twelve."

"Has anything like this ever happened to him before?"

"No"

"Have you ever seen this kind of rash on his back and sores like this on the back of his legs?"

"No, I've never seen anything like that on him."

The paramedic turned to his partner.

"Please contact Highland General and tell them to have a quarantine room set up. Tell them that we have a twelve year old male, running a fever with a rash that seems to be spreading rapidly on his back and legs. His breathing is shallow and has developed a cough since we been here. We will stabilize him for transport."

His mom heard all the paramedic said and began crying, repeating over and over: "My baby, my baby."

Mark heard bits and snatches of the radio communication between the paramedics and the hospital. Finally, he understood they were ready to transport Jason to the hospital. All the while, Mark prayed to Jesus, asking God to protect his brother and to help his mom and dad.

"Who are you talking to, Mark?" Donna asked.

"I am talking to Jesus," Mark told her.

Donna looked at Mark with a strange look on her face and asked Mark who in the world was Jesus. Is it someone that lives on our street or what?

Mark looked over at her and said that she would probably meet him in a couple of days and with that Donna seemed to be satisfied.

They were interrupted by their father.

"They're taking Jason to Highland General. I'm riding with him in the ambulance. Your mother will drive you two to the hospital."

Both Donna and Mark hugged their dad before he rushed out the door after Jason who lay on the stretcher now being pushed out the front door by the paramedics. Jason was covered in a blanket. Mark could see they had inserted tubes into Jason's nose, and had an IV in his arm at the wrist. Jason was still with eyes closed and silent. What concerned Mark most was the look on his parent's faces as they embraced and kissed quickly.

The sirens blared as the ambulance pulled out of the driveway and gained speed down their street, headed to the hospital.

Maria, Mark, and Donna scurried around, getting dressed and gathering a few things they might need. As she worked, Maria noted that she didn't hear Mark or Donna. What are they doing? Where were they? We have to hurry, she thought.

She walked towards Mark's room and opened the door. She was so surprised to find Mark, kneeling with his sister, hands folded, eyes toward the ceiling, whispering a prayer for Jason. She was moved to tears at the sight and slowly, quietly backed out the door and walked back to her own room to finish packing, all the while saying her own prayer.

"I am so proud of Mark and Donna," Maria whispered to God. "Jesus, we need you now."

A few minutes passed and there was a faint knock on her door. Maria opened the door to find Mark. He rushed in, grabbed his mom by the waist and told her, "Mom, I love you and dad so much. Don't worry. I really believe Jason is going to be okay."

"Mark, I want to thank you and your little sister for saying a prayer for Jason. Praying is something that is coming back into this house, regardless of how your dad feels—I promise you."

"Mom, that's awesome. Jesus is very nice and good. Do you believe that?"

"My dear Mark, you are such a sweet and loving child. I knew that you would be special even the night you were born. I know Jesus is very nice and good, but sometimes I have a very difficult time believing in Him because of what happened to your dad."

"But mom, dad didn't ask Jesus for help from his heart. That is why nothing happened."

Maria was shocked by Mark's revelation.

"Mom, I was scared to tell dad but when I spent the night with David's family, we went to church together. I loved it! It was so neat and there were so many happy people there. These people talk to Jesus and he speaks to them. Did you know that Jesus even died on a cross for us for OUR sins? He did nothing wrong. All He was here for was to teach us how to live together, love one another, to do no harm and to live with him forever in heaven."

Maria was moved incredibly by all that Mark said.

"Mark, you are making me so proud right now," she said.

"Mom there is something else I've been waiting to tell you, but I was a little worried that you might tell dad, and that he would blow up."

Donna joined them, needing some help with snaps and buttons. As Maria helped her dress, she responded,

"Mark, you can tell me anything. Don't keep things like that inside. Go ahead and tell me."

"Well mom, remember when you took me to the mall and I wandered off?"

"How in the world could I forget? I could just picture you dead in some ditch somewhere."

"You always warned me not to go off with anybody, regardless of how friendly they may seem. When you found me, I told you I had been talking to an older man. The man was sitting on the same bench I chose to sit on. The man spoke to me as if he knew our family very well—"

"In spite of all that Mark, you are still not to talk with or walk off with strangers. That is how children get picked up by bad people. It just so happened that this man wasn't bad. You were lucky. But go on."

"I know, I know. Well, he and I talked about many things, including how much he loved people and always did his best to get along with everyone but that a lot of people he loved simply ignored him. He also said that regardless of how they felt about him, he still loved them. He told me that God loves all of us and expects us to love everybody as we love ourselves. He told me that he heard you calling for me in the mall. He said I should stay there and that He would lead you to me. Then he told me the strangest thing. He said for me to remember that, 'God so loved the world that he sent his only son (Jesus) that whoever believes in Him will never die or go to hell, but will live forever in heaven, in everlasting life.' He said I would understand all He had said one day. He also promised I would teach these things to many others who don't believe, and that they would then believe. He said it would start with our family."

Maria's attention was riveted on her son.

Love of the Father

"What else did He say Mark?"

"That night, He came to me in a dream. He brought me to see grandma. He told me a lot. He is disappointed in dad leaving him. He said that dad believed he could do something to help him and grandpa save the business—and he was right—but that dad gave up on him too quickly. The biggest and scariest thing he said to me was that Jason would get very sick...and that only by dad trusting God would Jason recover."

Maria was at a total loss for words and very concerned about what she heard. But they had to hurry now.

"Mark thank you for sharing all of this. Let's keep talking about this after we get to the hospital and check on Jason."

She shooed both children toward the car, grabbing things up as she headed out the door. Within minutes they were headed to the hospital.

Maria could only think of Jason now. She whispered a prayer, "Oh Father, protect your children from harm; put your heavenly arms around me and walk with me through this time of trial. Protect those I love from any danger or sickness. Help me to stay close to you as I am surrounded by those who deny you or who have turned their backs on you. Let my faith grow and become strong. Heavenly Father, be with my family, forgive us of our wrongdoing and help us to love others as your son Jesus Christ loves us. Amen."

Chapter 8

A Family's Grief

Jason was alone with his firstborn son and namesake. It had been a harrowing hour or so for Jason. He sat in the hospital room, looking down at his son's motionless form and tears came to his eyes.

Why Jason Junior and not me? he wondered. His son had never done anything bad to anyone. He did not deserve this, though he himself had a long list of sins which deserved punishment. His tears began to flow. As he looked at his son lying there, with tubes in his nose, hooked up to equipment, all he could do was cry and wonder why.

Love of the Father

Jason watched through a window, as nurses came in to check Jason Juniors' vital signs or perform some test, then disappear as quickly as they had come. He had not seen the doctor in the room yet and that made him anxious. All Jason could do was watch as his son struggled for every breath.

He thought back to when Jason was born and how thrilled they had been. As a new dad, he was so proud to name his firstborn after himself.

He remembered the time Jason fell off his bike, scraping his knee and how much commotion that caused. He thought back to Jason's first day of school and how scared Jason was.

A sound from the hallway distracted Jason from his reverie. He heard children's voices and a voice that sounded like Maria's "shooshing" them. He turned to the door and in bounced Mark and Donna. Jason cried at the sight of them and hugged them close.

"I love you kids!"

"We love you too daddy," they chorused.

Walking over to the window, Donna asked, "Why can't we go in there and be with Jason?"

"Well honey," her dad said, "this is a very special room and they can take care of him better.

Maria joined Donna at the window.

"My baby, my darling baby, please come back to us."

Jason stood next to Maria, put his arm around her, and together they gazed silently at Jason, wondering what in the world had happened. The doctors were not sure what was wrong and were only treating his symptoms and analyzing test results.

Maria broke the silence

"Jason, is he going to be alright?" she asked.

Jason looked into Maria's eyes, cradled her face in his hands.

"I have no doubt that he will be alright."

A small voice interrupted their moment.

"Mommy? Daddy? Are you okay?"

Mark and Donna were standing, looking up at them. Maria realized that although part of her and Jason's heart was in their stricken firstborn, the other parts of their heart were standing beside them. Reaching down, both Maria and Jason took their younger children into their arms, hugging and kissing them.

After a few minutes, Mark seized an opportunity.

"Dad, the way I understand it, God helps you if you ask him, so why don't we ask him for help."

No sooner had Mark spoken the words than his dad turned to him, less sharply than normal, to say "Mark, son, it just doesn't do any good. I learned that a long time ago. And I forbid it."

The unfairness of his innocent son being stricken was just one more proof to Jason that God, if he was there, did not care. He was angry and God was an easy target for his venom.

"Why not just pray and try again?" Mark protested.

"You know why not Mark. I've told you many times and made myself perfectly clear on this. There is no way I will change my mind. That's final! Your brother is going to be just fine without God's help."

Mark looked at his mother for help but she remained silent. He was deeply hurt. He looked at his brother lying there, with tubes in his nose, hooked up to a machine, IV needle in arm. Tears filled his eyes.

Mark recalled what both his grandma and Jesus told him in his dreams. His brother was not going to get better unless his dad turned his life back over to God. But he saw no way that he would be able to convince his dad to do that. Maybe Jesus will help if I ask Him, he thought.

"Mom, I'm hungry," he said.

Alright Mark, I will take you and Donna down to the cafeteria and that way your dad can have some time alone with Jason. She kissed Jason softly on the cheek, grabbed Donna by the hand and they walked quietly out the door and walked over to the elevators. On the elevator they met a nice nurse who led them most of the way to the cafeteria.

"Mom, is Jason going to be alright?" Mark asked.

"I am sure he will. This hospital has the best doctors in the country," she said as she patted Mark on the head.

Donna looking up at her mom smiled with a look that told her that she knew that her mom was right. They had nothing to worry about because her mom said so.

"Mom," Mark asked, "if I say something about Jesus, you won't holler at me will you?"

"Of course not Mark," his mother said with a slight chuckle.

"You know how I said that Jesus talked to me and told me that it was up to dad if Jason was going to get better or not. Well, so far dad has not changed and I really don't know what else to do."

Maria stooped down do she could look Mark in the eye and drew him toward her.

"Jason IS going to be alright."

She gave him a big hug.

"Let's get something to eat. I am sure that will make you feel better."

Mark told his mom that he had to go to the restroom and excused himself from the table.

Just after Mark entered the restroom, a bright light filled it. He reached for the door but it seemed to have disappeared. He was alone in a place with nothing in it but bright light. Mark did the only thing he could think to do—kneel down and pray. He began to pour out his heart. It would take a miracle for his dad to come to God. Why on earth had Jesus put this responsibility on him? He was just a kid!

No sooner had he prayed this than he heard a familiar voice. It was a voice that he had heard several times over the last few weeks. He turned to see a figure in a white robe coming toward him—It was Jesus. He held his hands out to him.

Jesus wrapped Mark in his arms.

"Mark, you are truly a blessing to my father and he wants you to know that he is here for you. He will help you. I am here for you my son. Don't be afraid. Don't worry. Mark, as you know, your father has free will. Just be faithful to do your best. The rest is up to your father. My Father wants your father back, but he will not beg. This is all the time we have."

Jesus left as quickly and silently as He had come. Mark took care of his business and exited the restroom. He left there determined to do everything in his power to turn his dad back to God. Walking out of the bathroom Mark noticed that the time he was in the bathroom was very short according to the clock on the wall. He marveled at all that had happened in just a few minutes. He returned to the table.

"You'd better hurry up and eat before the food gets cold," his mother said.

Mark did what she asked knowing his mother did not want to be away from Jason for long.

When they returned to Jason's room, Mark's dad motioned for him and hugged him again.

"I love you very much Mark," his father said. "When Jason gets well, all three of us are going to take the boat out for a week and have some fun. Would that be fun?"

"That'd be great!" Mark exclaimed. Mark loved the boat but it had been a long time since they had used it. Mark also loved this moment with his dad.

Mark looked over at his brother in the bed and was suddenly gripped with a fear that he would never recover.

"Dad, suppose Jason doesn't get any better and he goes away like grandma did, and we never get to see him again?"

This shook both of his parents. His father was unable to respond, but his mother did.

"There is no way that will happen. Jason will be fine, just wait and see!"

Then she turned away so he could not see her shed a few tears.

Mark knew what they needed to do.

"Mom and dad, why don't we all say a prayer to Jesus and see what happens?"

Love of the Father

The minute the words came out of Mark' mouth, he knew that however right his words may be, his timing was wrong.

His father turned and looked him in the eye.

"Mark, where in the world did you come up with an idea like that? You know how I feel about this. I am not going to repeat it again. Do not bring this up again."

Mark was crushed and had no idea what to do.

"Maria," Jason said, "I'd like to talk to you out in the hallway I need to tell you something that is for our ears only."

Maria moved toward the door and then turned to tell Donna and Mark to stay seated; they would be right back.

Once out in the hallway Jason turned toward Maria with a solemn look.

"The doctor told me what they think is wrong with Jason. They came in right after you-all left to get something to eat. They will be back soon to speak with both of us. They are pursuing two things right now...anthrax poisoning or meningitis."

Maria felt like her knees would buckle. She was dizzy, but steadied herself by gripping the hallway safety rail.

"How would he come into contact with anthrax? If he has this, does that mean we might all be affected as well?"

"I know," said Jason, "but they have ruled that out. We would be showing symptoms by now. They are going to do a spinal tap tonight to see if he has meningitis. Let's not tell Mark or Donna until we find out for sure Jason said."

Walking back into the room Maria fought back tears and quickly hugged the children again.

She approached the window, peering through the glass at Jason. There was movement now, but it was because he was writhing in pain. For the first time since becoming a mother, there was nothing she could do for one of her children.

Love of the Father

As Maria watched him through the window, she heard Jason Junior let out a loud sound, after which his body went completely limp. She grabbed Jason who had come up beside her and he hung onto her— then she limp in his arms.

When Maria came to, Jason told her that a nurse and a doctor had come to Jason's room and revived him. The doctor, Dr. Richards, told him that they had ordered more tests. Still no diagnosis.

Chapter 9

The Man on the Bench

Jason walked out in the hallway, shaking his head, feeling scared to death over what had just taken place. Though he had maintained a cool exterior throughout the crisis, inside he was falling apart. It was a good time for him to be alone and have some private time to process all that was happening.

Instead of taking the elevator, Jason opted to get a little exercise and use the stairs. Aside from his concern about Jason, his mind was unusually tuned in to Mark and Donna and how they were handling the situation of Jason being sick. He marveled at how they were holding up. He thought of what Mark had said, about loving his brother and how much he would hate it if something happened to him. That was pretty deep for a ten year old.

Then he thought of Mark's current accounts of Jesus and dreams. Mark hadn't been to church. How did he know anything about Jesus? No friends of theirs talked of Jesus (that he knew of—except for maybe that kid David's family). So how did Mark acquire so much affection for Jesus all f a sudden? Why was he being pushy about prayer? How did he know of Jesus' death and why he died? Although it sounded like something he could have made up, it was the way that he described things that made Jason wonder.

Jason reached the last step in the stairwell and passed through the door to the first floor. He had been so deeply in thought he had no memory of the four floors he had passed. The first floor lobby was packed with people and he sought a place away from all the hustle and bustle. He started up a long hallway that seemed to go on forever. At the end of it was a glass door to the outdoors and to fresh air. He noticed it was turning dark outside. It seemed the perfect route for a reflective stroll or to find an empty bench and just sit quietly.

As he walked, Jason's mind turned back to his stricken son His sudden sickness had shaken Jason to his core. A wild thought entered his mind. Was Jesus getting back at him? He worked through that for a moment, thinking that it could be possible. Then a more pressing thought hit him—What if my son dies? A stab of fear went through him. He was in the midst of this thought when he passed through the door to the outside, saw an empty bench, and headed toward it.

Just before he reached the bench, an elderly man he had not seen sat down on the bench as well. It was the only bench.

"Excuse me," Jason sputtered. I didn't see you there.

"No worries," the elderly man said. "There's plenty of room for two!"

Love of the Father

Jason was fine sharing a bench but hoped the old-timer wasn't a talker.

Jason leaned forward, putting his elbows on his knees, his face in his hands. Just as he returned to his thoughts, the elderly man began talking.

"Hello, my name is Joe," he said, holding out his hand for a shake.

Jason, trying to be polite said, "Hi Joe, my name is Jason. It's a pleasure to meet you." Jason sized up his bench buddy quickly and held his hand back, opting for a nod. The man's clothing was dirty and he smelled badly. Jason felt bad and hoped the man wasn't offended. To his surprise the man simply smiled, seemingly not offended in the least.

"Well good to meet you Jason," the man said with a smile.

They sat in silence for a minute or two. Joe looked over at Jason who looked like he was carrying the world on his shoulders.

"Is everything okay?" Joe asked.

"I'm sorry, I have a lot on my mind," Jason responded foggily. "What did you say?"

"I am very sorry young man. I didn't mean to disturb you but you look so down. Is there anything I can do to help you?"

Jason glanced at Joe, in his dirty clothes, unshaven, and untidy appearance and chuckled, "I don't think you can help me, but I appreciate the offer."

When Joe spoke next, he spoke with authority and confidence.

"Jason, give me a few minutes and tell me what your problem is and I promise, you will leave here with a very different outlook on the situation."

Jason noticed the sudden change in Joe's voice and turned to face him directly. He was a little put off by the intrusion, but figured, OK, I'll tell the old man my problems.

"I will make you a deal," Joe said as he moved over closer to Jason, "you tell me yours and I will tell you mine."

Jason recounted the last twenty-four hours, primarily of Jason Junior's sudden bout with what was probably meningitis. But then he got into his assessment of himself as being not the best father in the world, and telling about Maria, Donna, and Mark. He told Joe how upset Maria was and how the other kids were handling it.

"My youngest son Mark has been having these dreams where he claims he talks to Jesus. He says Jesus takes him up to heaven and lets him walk around. He said he's even seen his grandma up there a couple times—my mom who passed away."

"There is nothing wrong with that," said Joe. "Children can create entire imaginary worlds in their minds."

"Well, it goes beyond beautiful heaven and gets very personal. Mark keeps telling me I should turn back to God, not only to save Jason's life, but to save my soul as well. He seems to know some stuff that only God would know."

"That is where my story will begin," said Joe. "But you go ahead and finish first."

Jason found Joe so easy to talk to, he became confessional.

"I turned away from God several years ago. Long story short, it had to do with mine and my father's business failing and my mother's death. Two HUGE things I prayed for and believed God to intervene in—He answered neither prayer. I realized that if I didn't just do it myself and take action, nothing would happen. There was no way I was going to lose my business and go back to the way it was before. I have a responsibility to provide for my family and if I were to lose everything, there would have been no way for me to take care of them. So now my youngest son Mark is telling me, "If we have all our money and don't have Jason, then what good is that?' He believes that as long as we turn to God, everything will be alright. I know differently. He just keeps pushing the issue."

Love of the Father

Joe smiled at Jason sympathetically and said, "Let me tell you about my oldest son and his birth. My wife and I were not married yet but we were engaged. We looked forward to the day when we would have our own home, kids—especially the kids. We never messed around with sex because we were committed to doing what was right before God. I loved Maria very much. She was not just beautiful in appearance, but had a beautiful heart. She was kind and gentle—everyone loved her."

"Pardon," Jason said, "so you had a wife named Maria as well?"

Joe nodded his head and continued on with his story.

"Anyway Maria and I tried and tried to have a child but it was to no avail because she never got pregnant. One night, she had a dream. In that dream she was told that she and I were going to have a baby. It was so real Maria said that it felt like it was not a dream at all, but was real.

"A few nights after Maria's dream, I had a dream as well. In it, I was told by a young man that Maria and I were to have a baby! It was the strangest experience of my life. I felt as if I was talking to that young man just as I am talking with you now. When I awoke, I told Maria about it. We were both so happy and excited about what God was going to do. We both now believed God would do it.

"It took me believing that God could and would do it that enabled us to be able to have a child, I truly believe. Ever since then, my wife and I have kept our faith in God and we have enjoyed so much love, peace, and happiness in life."

"So you had your child?" Jason asked.

"We had our son, Jacob nine months to the day after my dream!" he chuckled. "You know Jason; it seemed like a miracle for us. We had been trying for so long! Jacob grew into a bright young man. As he grew up, we really had to keep a close watch on him. He was a good boy although he was like any other child, getting into things and sometimes even trying to tell people what to do. He was such a gentle child and people he met seemed to just love him. He knew a lot at a young age, especially about Christianity because he was so knowledgeable about it and could relate it in such a way that people understood it as a relationship. He was so convincing that those who heard him believed in what he was saying. They believed he spoke God's word. They would always say how smart he was for his age and things like that.

"Jacob grew up and became a craftsman who worked in wood—beautiful creations. He built tables, chairs, cabinets, ornate wooden facades and pillars—you name it. His work was about as perfect as you can imagine. One day he came in and told us he had to go do God's work. We were shocked, but at the same time we were really proud.

"What did you tell him?" Jason asked.

"We told him to be careful and that he went with our blessing. Jacob had such a way with people that they came from near and far just to hear him talk about God and his love. He did so many good things for people. My son was a very simple, humble young man who always put other's feelings and well-being ahead of his own. If they were hungry he would feed them. He always seemed to have enough for everyone. He would help sick people that had no one to help them. Some he served by taking them to his own doctor. He always treated people with utmost love and respect, whether close friends or strangers — just as he was taught by his heavenly Father.

"Jacob was an extraordinary man when it came to getting people to follow him because his words went right to the heart of people. Their lives were changed by his words.

"Then one evening, he came to our home and told us that he was worried, that some other religious leaders seemed jealous of him and that they were starting trouble in some of the cities in which he ministered. He made especially sure that we knew he loved us very much that night. He told us not to worry, that if anything happened, it would not stop the work of God from continuing. This concerned us very much. It broke our hearts."

"I understand that," Jason said. "I would be worried to death if one of my sons told me people were trying to hurt him, just for doing God's work."

Joe smiled kindly at Jason.

"I learned a long time ago that worrying brings on nothing but more worry. And once again Maria and I realized we had to place our trust in God once again. You see Jason, Jacob was a strong believer in God and put his total trust in him. He taught us to do the same.

"Jacob traveled everywhere and touched the lives of many thousands of people. His message was simple, but life-changing. He would tell people the ways of God, the importance of believing Him and commanded them to love one another. He was faithful to his work and that message until the Lord called him up."

"Called him up?" Jason asked.

Joe's eyes watered as he looked Jason in the eye, saying, "A bunch of people who would not turn to God jumped on him, beat him, and killed him. My son was so special and so believed in the power of God that when he came into contact with those who didn't, he would push even harder to persuade them to believe. We loved our son very much and we would do anything to have him back. If only I would have known that then."

"Joe, that's horrible!" Jason said. "How did you ever recover from such a tragedy?

"It was hard. Shortly afterward, Maria and I started having problems and to stay away from facing them, I put a one hundred percent of my time into my work. Maria put her time into God and asked Him for help and strength."

"The way Maria looked at it was more of a blessing than a tragedy. Before he died, Jacob did a lot of good things for people. Many people were loyal to him and promised him they would carry on what he had begun. Maria wanted our son to do good, not only for himself, but for others. That was what happened and she was very proud of him for that.

"As for me, I turned to my money to help me by going out and gambling, drinking, and even looking at other women. I thought my money would never run out, but I was wrong. Soon the collectors came a-calling and I was paying out more then I was making. The money started to run short and I had to start laying people off and I soon found myself alone.

"The next part of my story isn't too pretty. I found myself on the street. I went from a married man with a beautiful wife and a son that could do no wrong, to a drunk on the street. You see Jason, God gave me two choices and I chose the latter."

Jason was moved by the story and took a minute to let it sink in. Then he remembered Joe had begun by saying the story he would share somehow reminded him of Jason's situation.

"Joe, you are using this story to tell me something, but I haven't quite pieced it together yet."

"Look at me Jason," Joe said with a tear in his eye and a fierce sincerity. "Your son Mark is totally right. The story I told you is very true, though there is much more to it. Mark is trying to tell you about the importance of believing in God. It was the same for us with our son. Listen to what your son is saying Jason. That is all I ask."

Jason sat for a moment in silence. Realizing his short walk had gone way long, Jason stood up to leave.

"Joe, you've got my attention. Thank you for telling me some of your story."

"I'm sure I'll see you around."

Jason turned and took a few steps, then decided to shake Joe's hand. When he turned, Joe was gone. There was no one in sight any direction he looked. It was as if Joe had disappeared into thin air.

Strange, very strange, Jason thought to himself. He turned and headed back into the hospital.

Jason made his way into elevator and quickly pushed the up button. The doors opened to the fifth floor and Jason stepped out into the hallway. As he

Love of the Father

began the long walk back to room 515, his mind reeled with the story Joe had shared with him. Mark's dreams, telling him he had to turn back to God, and Jason Junior being stricken with meningitis—there was definitely a message here. Jason thought he would collapse under the weight of it all.

Suddenly clarity came to his mind as he settled on one thing: He would talk with Mark and ask him exactly what Jesus had told him and what he was supposed to do.

Opening the door, he found Mark sitting alone, watching his brother. He gave Mark another big hug.

"I love you Mark. I want your brother to be well. I want our family to be like it was before, when everyone was happy and we did things together. To get there Mark, I'm pretty sure I need to talk to you about your dreams of Jesus and your grandma. I need to know everything, exactly what was said."

"I love you too dad...and you will be glad you asked, I promise."

Mark was on top of the world.

Chapter 10

The Conversation

Jason pulled the chair up next to Mark, looked him in the eyes and said, "Alright son, tell me about the dreams."

Mark looked at his dad, straightened himself in the chair, and began by telling of meeting the man in the mall.

"You know most of the story dad so I will tell you some of the things that I don't think you know. That man in the mall, he said he had many children. Just before mom found me, the man told me that he would be seeing me again the very night—and it happened! When I had my dream, the man who appeared to me looked exactly like the man I met in the mall. The closer he got, I recognized him and he smiled. It was the man—and he was Jesus! He told me I didn't know him because I had never been to church or prayed, or really heard much about him, but he knew me.

"He took me to His Father's house, heaven. It was so beautiful, peaceful, warm and loving there. Grandma was there and she was so happy I got to visit with her for a few minutes. You know dad, if that was heaven; that is where I want to go when I die. Everything was so clean and bright, the angels were singing and the people there were all smiling and happy. Then He told me that we had to go, and the next thing I knew I was back in my bed."

"Mark," his dad said, "are you positive that it was your grandma? And why do you think Jesus would pick you to see heaven...out of all the children in this world? You have never been to church, and I am sure there are many kids that go every Sunday."

"I asked him why he chose me and he told me that the Father chooses many children every day that don't go to church or worship him at all. He does this because they are the ones who are lost—he is trying to save them."

Mark's dad looked at him and shook his head as if to agree with his son.

"What about your grandmother? What did she look like? How did you know her?"

"Dad, she looked exactly the way she did when she was here. But it was a younger her...and she had a glow about her, like she was filled with light. She had a beautiful smile."

"Son, I am so glad you shared this with me and I will do what I can to try and change. You must really love your brother very much to come and face me with this after the way I always told you not to talk about God in the house. I love you son and I love Jason, Donna and your mother so very much."

"Dad, I love you too and I am so happy for you and proud of you for what you are going to do."

"You know son, what you are saying is starting to make a lot of sense to me but I want to hear the rest of the story."

Mark picked up where he left off.

"Jesus came to me again, in a dream. This time he took me to see his Father, well, what I could see of him. The light was so bright, I couldn't really see him. God told me that there was going to be sickness in the family, that it would be Jason, and that there was one person in the family who could save him—you. He told me that you had turned away from him, left him, and that really hurt him. He hates to lose any of his people and see them fall to the other side. He warned me that the devil is just waiting for people to do what you did—lose faith in Him. Dad, you can only save Jason by turning your life back over to God again."

"So, let me get this straight...in order to save Jason, I have to become a Christian again, and that is all?"

"He told me that you will be given choices. Some of them are choices of evil, put out there by the devil to lure the weak, while others are put out there by God to get you back on the good side. Dad, it's your choice. But what you decide has to come from the heart."

Mark looked at his dad with pleading eyes, "Dad, go to the chapel. Talk to Jesus and ask Him for help. I don't understand what happened with you and grandpa and why you both turned away from Jesus, but I know God is kind, loving, and forgiving. Jesus and his Father are waiting for you to ask them back into your life."

They heard familiar voices in the hallway. Maria and Donna were back. Jason and Mark rose to greet them.

Chapter 11

Jesus and the Dad

Maria and Donna walked into the room and giving Mark and Jason hugs along with hamburgers and fries.

"How is he doing?" Maria asked. "Is there any change?"

"No," Jason said. "He is about the same as he was but I have a strong feeling that he will be making a turn for the better soon."

Jason looked Maria in the eye and smiled.

"I am going to the chapel and pray. I am going to do something I should have done a long time ago. I love my son and if it takes going back to God then that is what I am going to do. Are you and the kids okay staying here?"

Maria smiled her okay.

Stepping out into the hallway, Jason made his way to the chapel. Jason was a little nervous. It had been a long time since he had set foot in a church or chapel. The hallway seemed to go on forever. Rounding the last curve, he looked up and saw the chapel sign. He opened the door and looked around. He was alone.

Jason made his way down to a pew not too far from the altar and quickly put the kneeler down, and there he knelt. He had not been there long when he heard a voice from behind him say, "Jason Albright, I have not seen you here in years."

Turning in the direction of the voice, Jason saw no one there. That's strange, he thought. After a minute, he resumed praying. Again he heard the voice but this time a little closer and more toward the front of the chapel.

"Jason! Look up. I am here."

Looking in the general direction, he still saw nothing.

The third time the voice was louder and unnerving.

"Jason! Look up! I am here."

Enough is enough, he thought. Now he looked all around him.

Suddenly, there was a still, soft voice that came from his right side.

"Jason, my son. Welcome back to the house of the Lord."

This was followed by a tap on his shoulder.

Turning, Jason saw a figure in a white robe in the midst of a light so bright it illuminated the figure completely. Jason had to shade his eyes from the light. When he dropped his hands, the man was standing beside him and spoke.

"Jason, my Father and I have been waiting for a long time, and are glad to see you here."

Jason was overwhelmed at the sight. In a shaking voice he asked, "You're not who I think you are, are you?"

"Who do you think I am Jason?"

"Jesus! My son Mark told me he had seen you in several dreams; your Father as well. He also told me that if I make the right choice that my oldest son will be spared. What must I do? I would do anything to save my son!"

"You must pray Jason and ask my Father to forgive you for turning your back on Him. He always loved you Jason and yet you put material things, your own wisdom and your own strength ahead of your faith and belief in him. From your heart, you must understand how wrong and foolish you have been. Not only must you ask the Father for forgiveness, you must show that you really mean it. He knows that you are a very loving, devoted father and husband. He also knows something about you that you have failed to tell your wife. The Father knows that you are a very sick man and that if He calls you to eternity now, there is no way He would let you into heaven. Pray Jason and listen to what He tells you."

Jason was broken. He knelt down on the kneeler, bowed his head, and began to pray.

"Oh Lord, you know my firstborn lies in this hospital, at death's door. Lord God, you know that I would do anything to save him. I know that I've disappointed you Lord, in my actions when I was losing my business, in how I reacted when you took my mother, in my lack of integrity in business, and in forbidding any mention of you in my home. Lord, I am sorry for all the wrong I have done and I beg your forgiveness."

Suddenly a voice spoke out. "Jason I know you love your family and that is why you did what you did, but there is no excuse for it. Your time on earth is limited. I will give you the choice—your life for his."

Jason was shocked by God's word and the choice he put before him. But he knew what he must do.

Love of the Father

"All I ask is, if possible, that I see Jason healthy one more time, that I hug my wife and kids one last time. Then I will gladly give my life for my son."

"Blessed are you, Jason Albright. Return to your family in room 515. Your son is awake and well."

Chapter 12

God's Promise Made Good

Jason dashed from the chapel, jumped into the elevator, and was soon walking the long hallway toward his son's room. Though he had no idea how long God would allow him to live, and that scared him, Jason's heart was at peace knowing his son was healed.

As he moved quickly through the hallway, tears rolled down Jason's cheeks. Some were tears of joy for the life of Jason and others were tears of sadness, that he would not share in the life of his children or grow old with his wife.

He was close to Jason's room, when two nurses and a doctor passed him in the hallway. He heard loud crying mixed with laughter. Pushing open the door, he saw Maria, Mark and Donna standing by Jason's bed, beaming. There was Jason, still in bed, but awake and smiling!

Honey, our son is alright!" Maria nearly screamed, as she leapt into his arms, grabbing him tightly around the neck.

A week after his sudden awakening, Jason was released from the hospital and the Albright family was in a steady state of celebration. The first Sunday morning following Jason's release, the Albright family rose early and headed to church. Mark and Jason had shared all that Jesus and his Father had spoken and done. The entire family couldn't wait to go to church.

As the months passed, Mark would still get unexpected visits from Jesus and he would talk to him about things going on in his life.

Love of the Father

There came a day when Jesus visited while Mark played one of the games in his room. Jesus told Mark to kneel by his bed and pray. Mark did exactly as he was told. It wasn't too long before there was a bright light and a voice from within the light calling to him.

"Mark, the Father wants me to share something very serious with you. First, he wants you to know that he is so proud of all you did to save your brother and father. As you know, he let your brother live and accepted your father back into his arms. God has been faithful to you. As you remain close to him, he will bless you throughout your life. You know the Father will do anything for you, don't you?"

"Thank you so much for all of that Jesus," Mark replied. You have always done what you promised me."

"Here is the second thing. You are going to have to trust me more than ever for what I am about to tell you. My Father is going to call your father into eternity soon, to be with us. Your father is very ill

Love of the Father

and will not be with you much longer. He knows this. We've already told him he is coming to us soon.

"When your brother lay dying in the hospital, your father visited us in the chapel. He was already sick. My Father gave him a choice—his life for your brother's life. Your father chose to give up his own life to save your brother. The only thing he wanted was to spend a little time with all of you before he was called and we agreed to that. The Father does not want you to be upset with him or your father. He loves you very much Mark and besides, your father will be with his mother again for all eternity. Do you understand Mark?"

Mark, with tears in his eyes, shook his little head yes and said, "I know dad will be happy with you and be happy there. He misses grandma."

Mark took the hand of Jesus. Very gently, Jesus pulled Mark to his chest.

"Mark Albright, you have done great deeds for the Father and he is very pleased with you. He will watch over your family and bless each of you greatly.

Love of the Father

I must go now Mark. The peace of My Father is with you."

Then he was gone.

Although Mark knew that he would miss his dad, he also knew that his dad would be in a much better place, with Jesus and his Father.

A few days had passed since the last time Jason had seen Jesus. He knew his time on earth was nearing its end and he had been totally devoted to his family for months now. They did as much in a day as they possibly could and, if possible, threw in something extra. They even took up bowling, something none of them knew anything about. All they knew was that it could be done together as a family and that is what really mattered. Sunday mass had become a normal activity since Jason's meeting with God.

One Sunday evening, it happened. The Albright family was all tucked in for the night. All had said their prayers and were at peace with Jesus. Jason turned over, closed his eyes, and whispered, "Sweet

Jesus, I love you and am ready to spend eternity with you," and closed his eyes.

No sooner had Jason closed his eyes when he encountered a bright light. From this light walked three figures, Jesus, his mother, and another he did not recognize.

"My dear, dear son," said Jesus, "the Father and I are so proud of you...and so is your mother."

Jason could not believe he was actually seeing his mother.

"Mom, Mark has told me all about meeting you and I am so glad you are happy—but I miss you. I know dad will be happy when his time comes and he will be able to spend eternity with you."

His mom looked at Jason with a loving smile and said, "Son, we are so proud of all that you did."

"What do you mean? What did I do?"

There was another flash of bright light and Jason heard familiar voices talking. The first voice he made out was Maria's, then his doctor's voice.

"Doctor, is Jason going to be alright?"

"He does have a blockage in two of his arteries, so this wasn't as bad as we suspected. But it is a warning to Jason that he simply must slow down."

The last thing he heard his doctor say was chilling, "We could have been talking about a death certificate if God had not given him a reprieve."

Maria Albright was up and dressed very early the next day, along with her three kids. They wanted to make early mass. Following that, they wanted to get to the hospital as early as possible, the kids to visit their dad, Maria to visit her husband, of whom she was very proud.

Epilogue

We all have some Jason Albright in us but we never face the fact that bad things can and will happen—that's just life. Because of that we must always strive to keep our relationship with God in the forefront of our lives. Most of us live with the idea that we don't need God in our lives at all and feel that if something bad comes about, we can handle it. As Jason Albright found out, that is just not true.

Although the Albright's company, Bright Idea did well all those years without Jason going to church or allowing his family to go to church, God had his eye on the family, waiting for the right moment to bring it to Him.

Love of the Father

God allows certain destructive things to happen in our lives, just as he did in the life of Job (though thankfully for most of us, not on that grand scale). No matter what comes, God is there, watching over us, seeing the choices that we make. Are we making choices that keep us pointed toward him, or do we make choices that point us away from him? As we stay pointed toward him, cling to him and refuse to let go, in due time, we will overcome through him.

So it was with Jason Albright, a man who had walked away from the church and made his family do the same thing. After Mark wandered away from his brother, met the man in the mall and had the dream, he was faced with a seemingly impossible task. He had no idea how his father would react to him talking about God, and encouraging his father to return to God. Mark came to understand that he was not to focus on the outcome, but on being faithful to do what God asked of him—no matter how impossible it seemed. As a result, Mark saw a miracle in his father's life.

Love of the Father

Jason's family consisted of wife Maria, eldest son Jason Junior, Mark, and the "baby, Donna. Although Jason loved his family, business had become his first love. It was because of the strong love affair with business and no love or time for God that God brought on a number of strange circumstances, not to hurt him, but to reveal the worst in him, so he would see his need for God and return to Him.